<u>VENGEANCE IS MINE</u>

BY

ALGERNON BLACKWOOD

British Library Cataloguing-in-Publication Data
A catalogue record for this book is available from
the British Library

Contents

Page
No.

Biography of Algernon Blackwood.......1

Vengeance is Mine....................................4

ALGERNON BLACKWOOD

Algernon Henry Blackwood was born in Shooter's Hill, South East England, in 1869. In his youth he trained as a doctor at Wellington College in Berkshire, and went on to pursue a number of careers, in areas as varied as milk farming, modelling, journalism and violin teaching. In his thirties, Blackwood returned to England from New York, where he had spent a number of years, and began to write stories of the supernatural.

Blackwood was extremely prolific, producing over the course of his life some ten original collections of short stories, fourteen novels, several children's books, and a number of plays. Most of his work was concerned with the ghostly, mythical or occult – themes which Blackwood was attracted to his whole life – and he is regarded as one of the earlier practitioners of 'weird fiction'. Amongst his best known short stories are 'The Wendigo', and 'The Willows' – a work which H. P. Lovecraft called "the finest weird story I have ever read." In 1914, he produced his short story collection *Incredible Adventures*, which leading literary critic

S. T. Joshi has said "may be the premier weird collection of this or any other century." Blackwood worked as an undercover agent for Britain during the First World War, and during the 1920s became famous for reading his ghost stories live on BBC radio and television.

After a number of strokes, Blackwood died in old age in Kent, England.

VENGEANCE IS MINE

Algernon Blackwood

I

An active, vigorous man in Holy Orders, yet compelled by heart trouble to resign a living in Kent before full middle age, he had found suitable work with the Red Cross in France; and it rather pleased a strain of innocent vanity in him that Rouen, whence he derived his Norman blood, should be the scene of his activities.

   He was a gentle-minded soul, a man deeply read and thoughtful, but goodness perhaps his out-standing quality, believing no evil of others. He had been slow, for instance, at first to credit the German atrocities, until the evidence had compelled him to face the appalling facts. With acceptance, then, he had experienced a revulsion which other gentle minds have probably also experienced – a burning desire, namely, that the perpetrators should be fitly punished.

   This primitive instinct of revenge – he called it a lust – he sternly repressed; it involved a descent to lower levels of conduct irreconcilable with the progress of the race he so passionately believed in. Revenge pertained to savage days. But, though he hid away the instinct in his heart, afraid of its clamour and persistency, it revived from time to time, as fresh horrors made it bleed anew. It remained alive, unsatisfied; while, with its analysis, his mind strove unconsciously. That an intellectual nation should deliberately include frightfulness as a chief item in its creed perplexed him horribly; it seemed to him conscious spiritual evil openly affirmed. Some genuine worship of Odin, Wotan, Moloch lay still embedded in the German outlook, and beneath the veneer of their pretentious culture. He often wondered, too, what effect the recognition of these horrors must have upon gentle minds in other men, and especially upon imaginative minds. How did they deal with the fact that this appalling thing existed in human nature in the twentieth century? Its survival, indeed, caused his belief in civilization as a whole to waver. Was progress, his pet ideal and cherished faith, after all a mockery? Had human nature not advanced . . . ?

His work in the great hospitals and convalescent camps beyond the town was tiring; he found little time for recreation, much less for rest; a light dinner and bed by ten o'clock was the usual way of spending his evenings. He had no social intercourse, for everyone else was as busy as himself. The enforced solitude, not quite wholesome, was unavoidable. He found no outlet for his thoughts. First-hand acquaintance with suffering, physical and mental, was no new thing to him, but this close familiarity, day by day, with maimed and broken humanity preyed considerably on his mind, while the fortitude and cheerfulness shown by the victims deepened the impression of respectful, yearning wonder made upon him. They were so young, so fine and careless, these lads whom the German lust for power had robbed of limbs, and eyes, of mind, of life itself. The sense of horror grew in him with cumulative but unrelieved effect.

With the lengthening of the days in February, and especially when March saw the welcome change to summer time, the natural desire for open air asserted itself. Instead of retiring early to his dingy bedroom, he would stroll out after dinner through the ancient streets. When the air was not too chilly, he would prolong these outings, starting at sunset and coming home beneath the bright mysterious stars. He knew at length every turn and winding of the old-world alleys, every gable, every tower and spire, from the *Vieux Marché*, where Joan of Arc was burnt, to the busy quays, thronged now with soldiers from half a dozen countries. He wandered on past grey gateways of crumbling stone that marked the former banks of the old tidal river. An English army, five centuries ago, had camped here among reeds and swamps, besieging the Norman capital, where now they brought in supplies of men and material upon modern docks, a mighty invasion of a very different kind. Imaginative reflection was his constant mood.

But it was the haunted streets that touched him most, stirring some chord his ancestry had planted in him. The forest of spires thronged the air with strange stone flowers, silvered by moonlight as though white fire streamed from branch and petal; the old church towers soared; the cathedral touched the stars. After dark the modern note, paramount in the daylight, seemed hushed; with sunset it underwent a definite night-change. Although the darkened streets kept alive in him the menace of fire and death, the crowding soldiers, dipped to the face in shadow, seemed somehow negligible; the leaning roofs and gables hid them in a purple sea of mist that blurred their modern garb, steel weapons, and the like. Shadows themselves, they entered the being of the town; their feet moved silently; there was a hush and murmur; the brooding buildings absorbed them easily.

Ancient and modern, that is, unable successfully to mingle, let fall grotesque, incongruous shadows on his thoughts. The spirit of mediæval days stole over him, exercising its inevitable sway upon a temperament already predisposed to welcome it. Witchcraft and wonder, pagan superstition and speculation, combined with an ancestral tendency to weave a spell, half of acceptance, half of shrinking, about his imaginative soul in which poetry and logic seemed otherwise fairly balanced. Too weary for critical judgment to discern clear outlines, his mind, during these magical twilight walks, became the playground of opposing forces, some power of dreaming, it seems, too easily in the ascendant. The soul of ancient Rouen, stealing beside his footsteps in the dusk, put forth a shadowy hand and touched him.

This shadowy spell he denied as far as in him lay, though the resistance offered by reason to instinct lacked true driving power. The dice were loaded otherwise in such a soul. His own blood harked back unconsciously to the days when men were tortured, broken on the wheel, walled up alive, and burnt for small offences. This shadowy hand stirred faint ancestral memories in him, part instinct, part desire. The next step, by which he saw a similar attitude flowering full blown in the German frightfulness, was too easily made to be rejected. The German horrors made him believe that this ignorant cruelty of olden days threatened the world now in a modern, organized shape that proved its survival in the human heart. Shuddering, he fought against the natural desire for adequate punishment, but forgot that repressed emotions sooner or later must assert themselves. Essentially irrepressible, they may force an outlet in distorted fashion. He hardly recognized, perhaps, their actual claim, yet it was audible occasionally. For, owing to his loneliness, the natural outlet, in talk and intercourse, was denied.

Then, with the softer winds, he yearned for country air. The sweet spring days had come; morning and evening were divine; above the town the orchards were in bloom. Birds blew their tiny bugles on the hills. The midday sun began to burn.

It was the time of the final violence, when the German hordes flung like driven cattle against the Western line where free men fought for liberty. Fate hovered dreadfully in the balance that spring of 1918; Amiens was threatened, and if Amiens fell, Rouen must be evacuated. The town, already full, became now over-full. On his way home one evening he passed the station, crowded with homeless new arrivals. "Got the wind up, it seems, in Amiens!" cried a cheery voice, as an officer he knew went by him hurriedly. And as he heard it the mood of the spring became of a sudden uppermost. He reached a decision. The German horror came abruptly closer. This further overcrowding of the narrow streets was more than he could face.

It was a small, personal decision merely, but he *must* get out among woods and fields, among flowers and wholesome, growing things, taste simple, innocent life again. The following evening he would pack his haversack with food and tramp the four miles to the great *Forêt Verte* – delicious name! – and spend the night with trees and stars, breathing his full of sweetness, calm and peace. He was too accustomed to the thunder of the guns to be disturbed by it. The song of a thrush, the whistle of a blackbird, would easily drown that. He made his plan accordingly.

The next two nights, however, a warm soft rain was falling; only on the third evening could he put his little plan into execution. Anticipatory enjoyment, meanwhile, lightened his heart; he did his daily work more competently, the spell of the ancient city weakened somewhat. The shadowy hand withdrew.

II

Meanwhile, a curious adventure intervened.

His good and simple heart, disciplined these many years in the way a man should walk, received, upon its imaginative side, a stimulus that, in his case, amounted to a shock. That a strange and comely woman should make eyes at him disturbed his equilibrium considerably; that he should enjoy the attack, though without at first responding openly – even without full comprehension of its meaning – disturbed it even more. It was, moreover, no ordinary attack.

He saw her first the night after his decision when, in a mood of disappointment due to the rain, he came down to his lonely dinner. The room, he saw, was crowded with new arrivals, from Amiens, doubtless, where they had "the wind up". The wealthier civilians had fled for safety to Rouen. These interested and, in a measure, stimulated him. He looked at them sympathetically, wondering what dear home-life they had so hurriedly relinquished at the near thunder of the enemy guns, and, in so doing, he noticed, sitting alone at a small table just in front of his own – yet with her back to him – a woman.

She drew his attention instantly. The first glance told him that she was young and well-to-do; the second, that she was unusual. What precisely made her unusual he could not say, although he at once began to study her intently. Dignity, atmosphere, personality, he perceived beyond all question. She sat there with an air. The becoming little hat with its challenging feather slightly tilted, the set of the shoulders, the neat waist and slender outline; possibly, too, the hair about the neck, and the faint perfume that was wafted towards him as the serving girl swept past, combined in the persuasion. Yet he felt it as more than a persuasion. She attracted him with a subtle vehemence he had never felt before. The instant he set eyes upon her his blood ran faster. The thought rose passionately in him, almost the words that phrased it: "I wish I knew her."

This sudden flash of response his whole being certainly gave – to the back of an unknown woman. It was both vehement and instinctive. He lay stress upon its instinctive character: he was aware of it before reason told him why. That it was "in response" he also noted, for although he had not seen her face and she assuredly had made no sign, he felt that attraction which involves also invitation. So vehement, moreover, was this response in him that he felt shy and ashamed the same instant, for it almost seemed he had expressed his thought in audible words. He flushed, and the flush ran through his body; he was conscious of heated blood as in a youth of twenty-five, and when a man past forty knows this touch of fever he may also know, though he may not recognize it, that the danger signal which means possible abandon has been lit.

Moreover, as though to prove his instinct justified, it was at this very instant that the woman turned and stared at him deliberately. She looked into his eyes, and he looked into hers. He knew a moment's keen distress, a sharpest possible discomfort, that after all he *had* expressed his desire audibly. Yet, though he blushed, he did not lower his eyes. The embarrassment passed instantly, replaced by a thrill of strangest pleasure and satisfaction. He knew a tinge of inexplicable dismay as well. He felt for a second helpless before what seemed a challenge in her eyes. The eyes were too compelling. They mastered him.

In order to meet his gaze she had to make a full turn in her chair, for her table was placed directly in front of his own. She did so without concealment. It was no mere attempt to see what lay behind by making a half-turn and pretending to look elsewhere; no corner of the eye business; but a full, straight, direct, significant stare. She looked into his soul as though she called him, he looked into hers as though he answered. Sitting there like a statue, motionless, without a bow, without a smile, he returned her intense regard unflinchingly and yet unwillingly. He made no sign. He shivered again. ... It was perhaps ten seconds before she turned away with an air as if she had delivered her message and received his answer, but in those ten seconds a series of singular ideas crowded his mind, leaving an impression that ten years could never efface. The face and eyes produced a kind of intoxication in him. There was almost recognition, as though she said: "Ah, there you are! I was waiting; you'll have to come, of course. You must!" And just before she turned away she smiled.

He felt confused and helpless.

The face he described as unusual; familiar, too, as with the atmosphere of some long forgotten dream, and if beauty perhaps was absent, character and individuality were supreme. Implacable resolution was stamped upon the features, which yet were sweet and womanly, stirring an emotion in him that he could not name and certainly did not recognize. The eyes, slanting a little upwards, were full of fire, the mouth voluptuous but very firm, the chin and jaw most delicately modelled, yet with a masculine strength that told of inflexible resolve. The resolution, as a whole, was the most relentless he had ever seen upon a human countenance. It dominated him. "How vain to resist the will," he thought, "that lies behind!" He was conscious of enslavement; she conveyed a message that he must obey, admitting compliance with her unknown purpose.

That some extraordinary wordless exchange was registered thus between them seemed very clear; and it was just at this moment, as if to signify her satisfaction, that she smiled. At his feeling of willing compliance with some purpose in her mind, the smile appeared. It was faint, so faint indeed that the eyes betrayed it rather than the mouth and lips; but it was there; he saw it, and he thrilled again to this added touch of wonder and enchantment. Yet, strangest of all, he maintains that with the smile there fluttered over the resolute face a sudden arresting tenderness, as though some wild flower lit a granite surface with its melting loveliness. He was aware in the clear strong eyes of unshed tears, of sympathy, of self-sacrifice he called maternal, of clinging love. It was this tenderness, as of a soft and gracious mother, and this implacable resolution, as of a stern, relentless man, that left upon his receptive soul the strange impression of sweetness yet of domination.

The brief ten seconds were over. She turned away as deliberately as she had turned to look. He found himself trembling with confused emotions he could not disentangle, could not even name; for, with the subtle intoxication of compliance in his soul lay also a vigorous protest that included refusal, even a violent refusal given with horror. This unknown woman, without actual speech or definite gesture, had lit a flame in him that linked on far away and out of sight with the magic of the ancient city's mediæval spell. Both, he decided, were undesirable, both to be resisted.

He was quite decided about this. She pertained to forgotten yet unburied things, her modern aspect a mere disguise, a disguise that some deep unsatisfied instinct in him pierced with ease.

He found himself equally decided, too, upon another thing which, in spite of his momentary confusion, stood out clearly: the magic of the city, the enchantment of the woman, both attacked a constitutional weakness in his blood, a line of least resistance. It wore no physical aspect, breathed no hint of ordinary romance; the mere male and female, moral or immoral touch was wholly absent; yet passion lurked there, tumultuous if hidden, and a tract of consciousness, long untravelled, was lit by sudden ominous flares. His character, his temperament, his calling in life as a former clergyman and now a Red Cross worker, being what they were, he stood on the brink of an adventure not dangerous alone but containing a challenge of fundamental kind that involved his very soul.

No further thrill, however, awaited him immediately. He left his table before she did, having intercepted no slightest hint of desired acquaintanceship or intercourse. He, naturally, made no advances; she, equally, made no smallest sign. Her face remained hidden, he caught no flash of eyes, no gesture, no hint of possible invitation. He went upstairs to his dingy room, and in due course fell asleep. The next day he saw her not, her place in the dining-room was empty; but in the late evening of the following day, as the soft spring sunshine found him prepared for his postponed expedition, he met her suddenly on the stairs. He was going down with haversack and in walking kit to an early dinner, when he saw her coming up; she was perhaps a dozen steps below him; they must meet. A wave of confused, embarrassed pleasure swept him. He realized that this was no chance meeting. She meant to speak to him.

Violent attraction and an equally violent repulsion seized him. There was no escape, nor, had escape been possible, would he have attempted it. He went down four steps, she mounted four towards him; then he took one and she took one. They met. For a moment they stood level, while he shrank against the wall to let her pass. He had the feeling that but for the support of that wall he must have lost his balance and fallen into her, for the sunlight from the landing window caught her face and lit it, and she was younger, he saw, than he had thought, and far more comely. Her atmosphere enveloped him, the sense of attraction and repulsion became intense. She moved past him with the slightest possible bow of recognition; then, having passed, she turned.

She stood a little higher than himself, a step at most, and she thus looked down at him. Her eyes blazed into his. She smiled, and he was aware again of the domination and the sweetness. The perfume of her near presence drowned him; his head swam. "We count upon you," she said in a low firm voice, as though giving a command; "I know . . . we may. We do." And, before he knew what he was saying, trembling a little between deep pleasure and a contrary impulse that sought to choke the utterance, he heard his own voice answering. "You can count upon me . . ." And she was already half-way up the next flight of stairs ere he could move a muscle, or attempt to thread a meaning into the singular exchange.

Yet meaning, he well knew, there was.

She was gone; her footsteps overhead had died away. He stood there trembling like a boy of twenty, yet also like a man of forty in whom fires, long dreaded, now blazed sullenly. She had opened the furnace door, the draught rushed through. He felt again the old unwelcome spell; he saw the twisted streets 'mid leaning gables and shadowy towers of a day forgotten; he heard the ominous murmurs of a crowd that thirsted for wheel and scaffold and fire; and, aware of vengeance, sweet and terrible, aware, too, that he welcomed it, his heart was troubled and afraid.

In a brief second the impression came and went; following it swiftly, the sweetness of the woman swept him: he forgot his shrinking in a rush of wild delicious pleasure.

The intoxication in him deepened. She had recognized him! She had bowed and even smiled; she had spoken, assuming familiarity, intimacy, including him in her secret purposes! It was this sweet intimacy, cleverly injected, that overcame the repulsion he acknowledged, winning complete obedience to the unknown meaning of her words. This meaning, for the moment, lay in darkness; yet it was a portion of his own self, he felt, that concealed it of set purpose. He kept it hid, he looked deliberately another way; for, if he faced it with full recognition, he knew that he must resist it to the death. He allowed himself to ask vague questions – then let her dominating spell confuse the answers so that he did not hear them. The challenge to his soul, that is, he evaded.

What is commonly called sex lay only slightly in his troubled emotions; her purpose had nothing that kept step with chance acquaintanceship. There lay meaning, indeed, in her smile and voice, but these were no handmaids to a vulgar intrigue in a foreign hotel. Her will breathed cleaner air; her purpose aimed at some graver, mightier climax than the mere subjection of an elderly victim like himself. That will, that purpose, he felt certain, were implacable as death, the resolve in those bold eyes was not a common one. For, in some strange way, he divined the strong maternity in her; the maternal instinct was deeply, even predominantly, involved; he felt positive that a divine tenderness, deeply outraged, was a chief ingredient too. In some way, then, she needed him, yet not she alone, for the pronoun "we" was used, and there were others with her; in some way, equally, a part of him was already her and their accomplice, an unresisting slave, a willing co-conspirator.

He knew one other thing, and it was this that he kept concealed so carefully from himself. His recognition of it was sub-conscious possibly, but for that very reason true: her purpose was consistent with the satisfaction at last of a deep instinct in him that clamoured to know gratification. It was for these odd, mingled reasons that he stood trembling when she left him on the stairs, and finally went down to his hurried meal with a heart that knew wonder, anticipation, and delight, but also dread.

III

The table in front of him remained unoccupied; his dinner finished, he went out hastily.

As he passed through the crowded streets, his chief desire was to be quickly free of the old muffled buildings and airless alleys with their clinging atmosphere of other days. He longed for the sweet taste of the heights, the smells of the forest whither he was bound. This *Forêt Verte*, he knew, rolled for leagues towards the north, empty of houses as of human beings; it was the home of deer and birds and rabbits, of wild boar too. There would be spring flowers among the brushwood, anemones, celandine, oxslip, daffodils. The vapours of the town oppressed him, the warm and heavy moisture stifled; he wanted space and the sight of clean simple things that would stimulate his mind with lighter thoughts.

He soon passed the *Rampe*, skirted the ugly villas of modern Bihorel and, rising now with every step, entered the *Route Neuve*. He went unduly fast; he was already above the Cathedral spire; below him the Seine meandered round the chalky hills, laden with war-barges, and across a dip, still pink in the afterglow, rose the blunt Down of Bonsecours with its anti-aircraft batteries. Poetry and violent fact crashed everywhere; he longed to top the hill and leave these unhappy reminders of death behind him. In front the sweet woods already beckoned through the twilight. He hastened. Yet while he deliberately fixed his imagination on promised peace and beauty, an undercurrent ran sullenly in his mind, busy with quite other thoughts. The unknown woman and her singular words, the following mystery of the ancient city, the soft beating wonder of the two together, these worked their incalculable magic persistently about him. Repression merely added to their power. His mind was a prey to some shadowy, remote anxiety that, intangible, invisible, yet knocked with ghostly fingers upon some door of ancient memory . . . He watched the moon rise above the eastern ridge, in the west the afterglow of sunset still hung red. But these did not hold his attention as they normally must have done. Attention seemed elsewhere. The undercurrent bore him down a siding, into a backwater, as it were, that clamoured for discharge.

He thought suddenly, then, of weather, what he called "German weather"–that combination of natural conditions which so oddly favoured the enemy always. It had often occurred to him as strange; on sea and land, mist, rain and wind, the fog and drying sun worked ever on *their* side. The coincidence was odd, to say the least. And now this glimpse of rising moon and sunset sky reminded him unpleasantly of the subject. Legends of pagan weather-gods passed through his mind like hurrying shadows. These shadows multiplied, changed form, vanished and returned. They came and went with incoherence, a straggling stream, rushing from one point to another, manoeuvring for position, but all unled, unguided by his will. The physical exercise filled his brain with blood, and thought danced undirected, picture upon picture driving by, so that soon he slipped from German weather and pagan gods to the witchcraft of past centuries, of its alleged association with the natural powers of the elements, and thus, eventually, to his cherished beliefs that humanity had advanced.

Such remnants of primitive days were grotesque super-stition, of course. But had humanity advanced? Had the individual progressed after all? Civilization, was it not the merest artificial growth? And the old perplexity rushed through his mind again – the German barbarity and blood-lust, the savagery, the undoubted sadic impulses, the frightfulness taught with cool calculation by their highest minds, approved by their professors, endorsed by their clergy, applauded by their women even – all the unwelcome, undesired thoughts came flocking back upon him, escorted by the trooping shadows. They lay, these questions, still unsolved within him; it was the undercurrent, flowing more swiftly now, that bore them to the surface. It had acquired momentum; it was leading somewhere.

They were a thoughtful, intellectual race, these Germans; their music, literature, philosophy, their science – how reconcile the opposing qualities? He had read that their herd-instinct was unusually developed, though betraying the characteristics of a low wild savage type – the lupine. It might be true. Fear and danger wakened this collective instinct into terrific activity, making them blind and humourless; they fought best, like wolves, in contact; they howled and whined and boasted loudly all together to inspire terror; their Hymn of Hate was but an elaboration of the wolf's fierce bark, giving them herd-courage; and a savage discipline was necessary to their lupine type.

These reflections thronged his mind as the blood coursed in his veins with the rapid climbing; yet one and all, the beauty of the evening, the magic of the hidden town, the thoughts of German horror, German weather, German gods, all these, even the odd detail that they revived a pagan practice by hammering nails into effigies and idols – all led finally to one blazing centre that nothing could dislodge nor anything conceal: a woman's voice and eyes. To these, he knew quite well, was due the undesired intensification of the very mood, the very emotions, the very thoughts he had come out on purpose to escape.

"It is the night of the vernal equinox," occurred to him suddenly, sharp as a whispered voice beside him. He had no notion whence the idea was born. It had no particular meaning, so far as he remembered.

"It had then . . ." said the voice imperiously, rising, it seemed, directly out of the under-current in his soul.

It startled him. He increased his pace. He walked very quickly, whistling softly as he went.

The dusk had fallen when at length he topped the long, slow hill, and left the last of the atrocious straggling villas well behind him. The ancient city lay far below in murky haze and smoke, but tinged now with the silver of the growing moon.

IV

He stood now on the open plateau. He was on the heights at last.

The night air met him freshly in the face, so that he forgot the fatigue of the long climb uphill, taken too fast somewhat for his years. He drew a deep draught into his lungs and stepped out briskly.

Far in the upper sky light flaky clouds raced through the reddened air, but the wind kept to these higher strata, and the world about him lay very still. Few lights showed in the farms and cottages, for this was the direct route of the Gothas, and nothing that could help the German hawks to find the river was visible.

His mind cleared pleasantly; this keen sweet air held no mystery; he put his best foot foremost, whistling still, but a little more loudly than before. Among the orchards he saw the daisies glimmer. Also, he heard the guns, a thudding concussion in the direction of the coveted Amiens, where, some sixty miles as the crow flies, they roared their terror into the calm evening skies. He cursed the sound, in the town below it was not audible. Thought jumped then to the men who fired them, and so to the prisoners who worked on the roads outside the hospitals and camps he visited daily. He passed them every morning and night, and the NCO invariably saluted his Red Cross uniform, a salute he returned, when he could not avoid it, with embarrassment.

One man in particular stood out clearly in this memory; he had exchanged glances with him, noted the expression of his face, the number of his gang printed on coat and trousers – "82". The fellow had somehow managed to establish a relationship; he would look up and smile or frown; if the news, from his point of view, was good, he

smiled; if it was bad, he scowled; once, insolently enough
– when the Germans had taken Albert, Péronne, Bapaume
– he grinned.

Something about the sullen, close-cropped face, typically
Prussian, made the other shudder. It was the visage of
an animal, neither evil nor malignant, even good-natured
sometimes when it smiled, yet of an animal that could be
fierce with the lust of happiness, ferocious with delight.
The sullen savagery of a human wolf lay in it somewhere.
He pictured its owner impervious to shame, to normal
human instinct as civilized people know these. Doubtless
he read his own feelings into it. He could imagine the
man doing anything and everything, regarding chivalry
and sporting instinct as proof of fear or weakness. He
could picture this member of the wolfpack killing a woman
or a child, mutilating, cutting off little hands even, with the
conscientious conviction that it was right and sensible to
destroy *any* individual of an enemy tribe. It was, to him,
an atrocious and inhuman face.

It now cropped up with unpleasant vividness, as he
listened to the distant guns and thought of Amiens with
its back against the wall, its inhabitants flying –

Ah! Amiens . . . ! He again saw the woman staring into
his obedient eyes across the narrow space between the
tables. He smelt the delicious perfume of her dress and
person on the stairs. He heard her commanding voice,
her very words: "We count on you . . . I know we can
. . . we do." And her background was of twisted streets,
dark alley-ways and leaning gables . . .

He hurried, whistling loudly an air that he invented
suddenly, using his stick like a golf club at every loose stone
his feet encountered, making as much noise as possible. He
told himself he was a parson and a Red Cross worker.
He looked up and saw that the stars were out. The pace
made him warm, and he shifted his haversack to the other
shoulder. The moon, he observed, now cast his shadow
for a long distance on the sandy road.

After another mile, while the air grew sharper and

twilight surrendered finally to the moon, the road began to curve and dip, the cottages lay farther out in the dim fields, the farms and barns occurred at longer intervals. A dog barked now and again; he saw cows lying down for the night beneath shadowy fruit-trees. And then the scent in the air changed slightly, and a darkening of the near horizon warned him that the forest had come close.

This was an event. Its influence breathed already a new perfume; the shadows from its myriad trees stole out and touched him. Ten minutes later he reached its actual frontier cutting across the plateau like a line of sentries at attention. He slowed down a little. Here, within sight and touch of his long-desired objective, he hesitated. It stretched, he knew from the map, for many leagues to the north, uninhabited, lonely, the home of peace and silence; there were flowers there, and cool sweet spaces where the moonlight fell. Yet here, within scent and touch of it, he slowed down a moment to draw breath. A forest on the map is one thing; visible before the eyes when night has fallen, it is another. It is real.

The wind, not noticeable hitherto, now murmured towards him from the serried trees that seemed to manufacture darkness out of nothing. This murmur hummed about him. It enveloped him. Piercing it, another sound that was not the guns just reached him, but so distant that he hardly noticed it. He looked back. Dusk suddenly merged in night. He stopped.

"How practical the French are," he said to himself – aloud – as he looked at the road running straight as a ruled line into the heart of the trees. "They waste no energy, no space, no time. Admirable!"

It pierced the forest like a lance, tapering to a faint point in the misty distance. The trees ate its undeviating straightness as though they would smother it from sight, as though its rigid outline marred their mystery. He admired the practical makers of the road, yet sided, too, with the poetry of the trees. He stood there staring, waiting, dawdling . . . About him, save for this murmur of the wind, was silence. Nothing living stirred. The world lay extraordinarily still. That other distant sound had died away.

He lit his pipe, glad that the match blew out and the damp tobacco needed several matches before the pipe drew properly. His puttees hurt him a little, he stooped to loosen them. His haversack swung round in front as he straightened up again, he shifted it laboriously to the other shoulder. A tiny stone in his right boot caused irritation. Its removal took a considerable time, for he had to sit down, and a log was not at once forthcoming. Moreover, the laces gave him trouble, and his fingers had grown thick with heat and the knots were difficult to tie . . .

"There!" He said it aloud, standing up again. "Now, at last, I'm ready!" Then added a mild imprecation, for his pipe had gone out while he stooped over the recalcitrant boot, and it had to be lighted once again. "Ah!" he gasped finally with a sigh as, facing the forest for the third time, he shuffled his tunic straight, altered his haversack once more, changed his stick from the right hand to the left – and faced the foolish truth without further pretence.

He mopped his forehead carefully, as though at the same time trying to mop away from his mind a faint anxiety, a very faint uneasiness, that gathered there. Was someone standing near him? Had somebody come close? He listened intently. It was the blood singing in his ears, of course, that curious distant noise. For, truth to tell, the loneliness bit just below the surface of what he found enjoyable. It seemed to him that somebody was coming, someone he could not see, so that he looked back over his shoulder once again, glanced quickly right and left, then peered down the long opening cut through the woods in front – when there came suddenly a roar and a blaze of dazzling light from behind, so instantaneously that he barely had time to obey the instinct of self-preservation and step aside. He actually leapt. Pressed against the hedge, he saw a motor-car rush past him like a whirlwind, flooding the sandy road with fire; a second followed it; and, to his complete amazement, then, a third.

They were powerful, private cars, so-called. This struck him instantly. Two other things he noticed, as they dived down the throat of the long white road – they showed no tail-lights. This made him wonder. And, secondly, the drivers, clearly seen, were women. They were not even in uniform – which made him wonder even more. The occupants, too, were women. He caught the outline of toque and feather – or was it flowers? – against the closed windows in the moonlight as the procession rushed past him.

He felt bewildered and astonished. Private motors were rare, and military regulations exceedingly strict; the danger of spies dressed in French uniform was constant; cars armed with machine guns, he knew, patrolled the countryside in all directions. Shaken and alarmed, he thought of favoured persons fleeing stealthily by night, of treachery, disguise and swift surprise; he thought of various things as he stood peering down the road for ten minutes after all sight and sound of the cars had died away. But no solution of the mystery occurred to him. Down the white throat the motors vanished. His pipe had gone out; he lit it, and puffed furiously.

His thoughts, at any rate, took temporarily a new direction now. The road was not as lonely as he had imagined. A natural reaction set in at once, and this proof of practical, modern life banished the shadows from his mind effectually. He started off once more, oblivious of his former hesitation. He even felt a trifle shamed and foolish, pretending that the vanished mood had not existed. The tobacco had been damp. His boot had really hurt him . . .

Yet bewilderment and surprise stayed with him. The swiftness of the incident was disconcerting; the cars arrived and vanished with such extraordinary rapidity; their noisy irruption into this peaceful spot seemed incongruous; they roared, blazed, rushed and disappeared; silence resumed its former sway.

But the silence persisted, whereas the noise was gone.

This touch of the incongruous remained with him as he now went ever deeper into the heart of the quiet forest. This odd incongruity of dreams remained.

V

The keen air stole from the woods, cooling his body and his mind; anemones gleamed faintly among the brushwood, lit by the pallid moonlight. There were beauty, calm and silence, the slow breathing of the earth beneath the comforting sweet stars. War, in this haunt of ancient peace, seemed an incredible anachronism. His thoughts turned to gentle happy hopes of a day when the lion and the lamb would yet lie down together, and a little child would lead them without fear. His soul dwelt with peaceful longings and calm desires.

He walked on steadily, until the inflexible straightness of the endless road began to afflict him, and he longed for a turning to the right or left. He looked eagerly about him for a woodland path. Time mattered little; he could wait for the sunrise and walk home "beneath the young grey dawn"; he had food and matches, he could light a fire, and sleep – No! – after all, he would not light a fire, perhaps; he might be accused of signalling to hostile aircraft, or a *garde forestière* might catch him. He would not bother with a fire. The night was warm, he could enjoy himself and pass the time quite happily without artificial heat; probably he would need no sleep at all . . . And just then he noticed an opening on his right, where a seductive pathway led in among the trees. The moon, now higher in the sky, lit this woodland trail enticingly; it seemed the very opening he had looked for, and with a thrill of pleasure he at once turned down it, leaving the ugly road behind him with relief.

The sound of his footsteps hushed instantly on the leaves and moss; the silence became noticeable; an unusual stillness followed; it seemed that something in his mind was also hushed. His feet moved stealthily, as though anxious to conceal his presence from surprise. His steps dragged purposely; their rustling through the thick dead leaves, perhaps, was pleasant to him. He was not sure.

The path opened presently into a clearing where the moonlight made a pool of silver, the surrounding brushwood fell away; and in the centre a gigantic outline rose. It was, he saw, a beech tree that dwarfed the surrounding forest by its grandeur. Its bulk loomed very splendid against the sky, a faint rustle just audible in its myriad tiny leaves. Dipped in the moonlight, it had such majesty of proportion, such symmetry, that he stopped in admiration. It was, he saw, a multiple tree, five stems springing with attempted spirals out of an enormous trunk; it was immense; it had a presence, the space framed it to perfection. The clearing, evidently, was a favourite resting-place for summer picnickers, a playground, probably, for city children on holiday afternoons; woodcutters, too, had been here recently, for he noticed piled brushwood ready to be carted. It indicated admirably, he felt, the limits of his night expedition. Here he would rest awhile, eat his late supper, sleep perhaps round a small – No! again – a fire he need *not* make; a spark might easily set the woods ablaze, it was against both forest and military regulations. This idea of a fire, otherwise so natural, was distasteful, even repugnant, to him. He wondered a little why it recurred. He noticed this time, moreover, something unpleasant connected with the suggestion of a fire, something that made him shrink; almost a ghostly dread lay hidden in it.

This startled him. A dozen excellent reasons, supplied by his brain, warned him that a fire was unwise; but the true reason, supplied by another part of him, concealed itself with care, as though afraid that reason might detect its nature and fix the label on. Disliking this reminder of his earlier mood, he moved forward into the clearing, swinging his stick aggressively and whistling. He approached the tree, where a dozen thick roots dipped into the earth. Admiring, looking up and down, he paced slowly round its prodigious girth, then stood absolutely still. His heart stopped abruptly, his blood became congealed. He saw something that filled him with a sudden emptiness of terror. On this western side the shadow lay very black; it was between the thick limbs, half stem, half root, where the dark hollows gave easy hiding-places, that he was positive he detected movement. A portion of the trunk had moved.

He stood stock still and stared – not three feet from the trunk – when there came a second movement. Concealed in the shadows there crouched a living form. The movement defined itself immediately. Half reclining, half standing, a living being pressed itself close against the tree, yet fitting so neatly into the wide scooped hollows, that it was scarcely distinguishable from its ebony background. But for the chance movement he must have passed it undetected. Equally, his outstretched fingers might have touched it. The blood rushed from his heart, as he saw this second movement.

Detaching itself from the obscure background, the figure rose and stood before him. It swayed a little, then stepped out into the patch of moonlight on his left. Three feet lay between them. The figure then bent over. A pallid face with burning eyes thrust forward and peered straight into his own.

The human being was a woman. The same instant he recognized the eyes that had stared him out of countenance in the dining-room two nights ago. He was petrified. She stared him out of countenance now.

And, as she did so, the under-current he had tried to ignore so long swept to the surface in a tumultuous flood, obliterating his normal self. Something elaborately built up in his soul by years of artificial training collapsed like a house of cards, and he knew himself undone.

"They've got me . . . !" flashed dreadfully through his mind. It was, again, like a message delivered in a dream where the significance of acts performed and language uttered, concealed at the moment, is revealed much later only.

"After all – they've got me . . . !"

VI

The dialogue that followed seemed strange to him only when looking back upon it. The element of surprise again was negligible if not wholly absent, but the incongruity of dreams, almost of nightmare, became more marked. Though the affair was unlikely, it was far from incredible. So completely were this man and woman involved in some purpose common to them both that their talk, their meeting, their instinctive sympathy at the time seemed natural. The same stream bore them irresistibly towards the same far sea. Only, as yet, this common purpose remained concealed. Nor could he define the violent emotions that troubled him. Their exact description was in him, but so deep that he could not draw it up. Moonlight lay upon his thought, merging clear outlines.

Divided against himself, the cleavage left no authoritative self in control; his desire to take an immediate decision resulted in a confused struggle, where shame and pleasure, attraction and revulsion mingled painfully. Incongruous details tumbled helter-skelter about his mind: for no obvious reason, he remembered again his Red Cross uniform, his former holy calling, his nationality too; he was a servant of mercy, a teacher of the love of God; he was an English gentleman. Against which rose other details, as in opposition, holding just beyond the reach of words, yet rising, he recognized well enough, from the bed-rock of the human animal, whereon a few centuries have imposed the thin crust of refinement men call civilization. He was aware of joy and loathing.

In the first few seconds he knew the clash of a dreadful fundamental struggle, while the spell of this woman's strange enchantment poured over him, seeking the reconciliation he himself could not achieve. Yet the reconciliation *she* sought meant victory or defeat; no compromise lay in it. Something imperious emanating from her already dominated the warring elements towards a coherent whole. He stood before her, quivering with emotions he dared not name. Her great womanhood he recognized, acknowledging obedience to her undisclosed intentions. And this idea of coming surrender terrified him. Whence came, too, that queenly touch about her that made him feel he should have sunk upon his knees?

The conflict resulted in a curious compromise. He raised his hand; he saluted; he found very ordinary words.

"You passed me only a short time ago," he stammered, "in the motors. There were others with you –"

"Knowing that you would find us and come after. We count on your presence and your willing help." Her voice was firm as with unalterable conviction. It was persuasive too. He nodded, as though acquiescence seemed the only course.

"We need your sympathy; we must have your power too."

He bowed again. "My power!" Something exulted in him. But he murmured only. It was natural, he felt; he gave consent without a question.

Strange words he both understood and did not understand. Her voice, low and silvery, was that of a gentle, cultured woman, but command rang through it with a clang of metal, terrible behind the sweetness. She moved a little closer, standing erect before him in the moonlight, her figure borrowing something of the great tree's majesty behind her. It was incongruous, this gentle and yet sinister air she wore. Whence came, in this calm peaceful spot, the suggestion of a wild and savage background to her? Why were there tumult and oppression in his heart, pain, horror, tenderness and mercy, mixed beyond disentanglement? Why did he think already, but helplessly, of escape, yet at the same time burn to stay? Whence came again, too, a certain queenly touch he felt in her?

"The gods have brought you," broke across his turmoil in a half whisper whose breath almost touched his face. "You belong to us."

The deeps rose in him. Seduced by the sweetness and the power, the warring divisions in his being drew together. His under-self more and more obtained the mastery she willed. Then something in the French she used flickered across his mind with a faint reminder of normal things again.

"Belgian –" he began, and then stopped short, as her instant rejoinder broke in upon his halting speech and petrified him. In her voice sang that triumphant tenderness that only the feminine powers of the Universe may compass: it seemed the sky sang with her, the mating birds, wild flowers, the south wind and the running streams. All these, even the silver birches, lent their fluid, feminine undertones to the two pregnant words with which she interrupted him and completed his own unfinished sentence:

"– and mother."

With the dreadful calm of an absolute assurance, she stood and watched him.

His understanding already showed signs of clearing. She stretched her hands out with a passionate appeal, a yearning gesture, the eloquence of which should explain all that remained unspoken. He saw their grace and symmetry, exquisite in the moonlight, then watched them fold together in an attitude of prayer. Beautiful mother hands they were; hands made to smooth the pillows of the world, to comfort, bless, caress, hands that little children everywhere must lean upon and love – perfect symbol of protective, self-forgetful motherhood.

This tenderness he noted; he noted next – the strength. In the folded hands he divined the expression of another great world-power, fulfilling the implacable resolution of the mouth and eyes. He was aware of relentless purpose, more – of merciless revenge, as by a protective motherhood outraged beyond endurance. Moreover, the gesture held appeal; these hands, so close that their actual perfume reached him, sought his own in help. The power in himself as man, as male, as father – this was required of him in the fulfilment of the unknown purpose to which this woman summoned him. His understanding cleared still more.

The couple faced one another, staring fixedly beneath the giant beech that overarched them. In the dark of his eyes, he knew, lay growing terror. He shivered, and the shiver passed down his spine, making his whole body tremble. There stirred in him an excitement he loathed, yet welcomed, as the primitive male in him, answering the summons, reared up with instinctive, dreadful glee to shatter the bars that civilization had so confidently set upon its freedom. A primal emotion of his under-being, ancient lust that had too long gone hungry and unfed, leaped towards some possible satisfaction. It was incredible; it was, of course, a dream. But judgment wavered; increasing terror ate his will away. Violence and sweetness, relief and degradation, fought in his soul, as he trembled before a power that now slowly mastered him. This glee and loathing formed their ghastly partnership. He could have strangled the woman where she stood. Equally, he could have knelt and kissed her feet.

The vehemence of the conflict paralysed him.

"A mother's hands . . ." he murmured at length, the words escaping like bubbles that rose to the surface of a seething cauldron and then burst.

And the woman smiled as though she read his mind and saw his little trembling. The smile crept down from the eyes towards the mouth; he saw her lips part slightly; he saw her teeth.

But her reply once more transfixed him. Two syllables she uttered in a voice of iron:

"Louvain."

The sound acted upon him like a Word of Power in some Eastern fairy tale. It knit the present to a past that he now recognized could never die. Humanity had *not* advanced. The hidden source of his secret joy began to glow. For this woman focused in him passions that life had hitherto denied, pretending they were atrophied, and the primitive male, the naked savage rose up, with glee in its lustful eyes and blood upon its lips. Acquired civilization, a pitiful mockery, split through its thin veneer and fled.

"Belgian . . . Louvain . . . Mother . . ." he whispered, yet astonished at the volume of sound that now left his mouth. His voice had a sudden fullness. It seemed a cave-man roared the words.

She touched his hand, and he knew a sudden intensification of life within him; immense energy poured through his veins; a mediæval spirit used his eyes; great pagan instincts strained and urged against his heart, against his very muscles. He longed for action. -

And he cried aloud: "I am with you, with you to the end!"

Her spell had vivified beyond all possible resistance that primitive consciousness which is ever the bed-rock of the human animal.

A racial memory, inset against the forest scenery, flashed suddenly through the depths laid bare. Below a sinking moon dark figures flew in streaming lines and groups; tormented cries went down the wind; he saw torn, blasted trees that swayed and rocked; there was a leaping fire, a gleaming knife, an altar. He saw a sacrifice.

It flashed away and vanished. In its place the woman stood, with shining eyes fixed on his face, one arm outstretched, one hand upon his flesh. She shifted slightly, and her cloak swung open. He saw clinging skins wound closely about her figure; leaves, flowers and trailing green hung from her shoulders, fluttering down the lines of her triumphant physical beauty. There was a perfume of wild roses, incense, ivy bloom, whose subtle intoxication drowned his senses. He saw a sparkling girdle round the waist, a knife thrust through it tight against the hip. And his secret joy, the glee, the pleasure of some unlawful and unholy lust leaped through his blood towards the abandonment of satisfaction.

The moon revealed a glimpse, no more. An instant he saw her thus, half savage and half sweet, symbol of primitive justice entering the present through the door of vanished centuries.

The cloak swung back again, the outstretched hand withdrew, but from a world he knew had altered.

To-day sank out of sight. The moon shone pale with terror and delight on Yesterday.

VII

Across this altered world a faint new sound now reached his ears, as though a human wail of anguished terror trembled and changed into the cry of some captured helpless animal. He thought of a wolf apart from the comfort of its pack, savage yet abject. The despair of a last appeal was in the sound. It floated past, it died away. The woman moved closer suddenly.

"All is prepared," she said, in the same low, silvery voice; "we must not tarry. The equinox is come, the tide of power flows. The sacrifice is here; we hold him fast. We only awaited you." Her shining eyes were raised to his. "Your soul is with us now?" she whispered.

"My soul is with you."

"And midnight," she continued, "is at hand. We use, of course, their methods. Henceforth the gods – their old-world gods – shall work on our side. They demand a sacrifice, and justice has provided one."

His understanding cleared still more then; the last veil of confusion was drawing from his mind. The old, old names went thundering through his consciousness – Odin, Wotan, Moloch – accessible ever to invocation and worship of the rightful kind. It seemed as natural as though he read in his pulpit the prayer for rain, or gave out the hymn for those at sea. That was merely an empty form, whereas this was real. Sea, storm and earthquake, all natural activities, lay under the direction of those elemental powers called the gods. Names changed, the principle remained.

"Their weather shall be ours," he cried, with sudden passion, as a memory of unhallowed usages he had thought erased from life burned in him; while, stranger still, resentment stirred – revolt – against the system, against the very deity he had worshipped hitherto. For these had never once interfered to help the cause of right; their feebleness was now laid bare before his eyes. And a twofold lust rose in him. "Vengeance is ours!" he cried in a louder voice, through which this sudden loathing of the cross poured hatred. "Vengeance and justice! Now bind the victim! Bring on the sacrifice!"

"He is already bound." And as the woman moved a little, the curious erection behind her caught his eye – the piled brushwood he had imagined was the work of woodmen, picnickers, or playing children. He realized its true meaning.

It now delighted and appalled him. Awe deepened in him, a wind of ice passed over him. Civilization made one more fluttering effort. He gasped, he shivered; he tried to speak. But no words came. A thin cry, as of a frightened child, escaped him.

"It is the only way," the woman whispered softly. "We steal from them the power of their own deities." Her head flung back with a marvellous gesture of grace and power; she stood before him a figure of perfect womanhood, gentle and tender, yet at the same time alive and cruel with the passions of an ignorant and savage past. Her folded hands were clasped, her face turned heavenwards. "I am a mother," she added, with amazing passion, her eyes glistening in the moonlight with unshed tears. "We all" – she glanced towards the forest, her voice rising to a wild and poignant cry – "all, all of us are mothers!"

It was then the final clearing of his understanding happened, and he realized his own part in what would follow. Yet before the realization he felt himself not merely ineffective, but powerless. The struggling forces in him were so evenly matched that paralysis of the will resulted. His dry

lips contrived merely a few words of confused and feeble
protest.

"Me!" he faltered. "My help –?"

"Justice," she answered; and though softly uttered, it
was as though the mediæval towers clanged their bells.
That secret, ghastly joy again rose in him; admiration,
wonder, desire followed instantly. A fugitive memory of
Joan of Arc flashed by, as with armoured wings, upon the
moonlight. Some power similarly heroic, some purpose
similarly inflexible, emanated from this woman, the savour
of whose physical enchantment, whose very breath, rose to
his brain like incense. Again he shuddered. The spasm of
secret pleasure shocked him. He sighed. He felt alert, yet
stunned.

Her words went down the wind between them:

"You are so weak, you English," he heard her terrible
whisper, "so nobly forgiving, so fine, yet so forgetful. You
refuse the weapon *they* place within your hands." Her face
thrust closer, the great eyes blazed upon him. "If we would
save the children" – the voice rose and fell like wind – "we
must worship where they worship, we must sacrifice to
their savage deities . . ."

The stream of her words flowed over him with this
nightmare magic that seemed natural, without surprise.
He listened, he trembled, and again he sighed. Yet in his
blood there was sudden roaring.

" . . . Louvain . . . the hands of little children . . . we have
the proof," he heard, oddly intermingled with another set of
words that clamoured vainly in his brain for utterance; "the
diary in his own handwriting, his gloating pleasure . . . the
little, innocent hands . . ."

"Justice is mine!" rang through some fading region of
his now fainting soul, but found no audible utterance.

" . . . Mist, rain and wind . . . the gods of German Weather
. . . We all . . . are mothers . . ."

"I will repay," came forth in actual words, yet so low he
hardly heard the sound. But the woman heard.

"We!" she cried fiercely, "*we* will repay!"

"God!" The voice seemed torn from his throat. "Oh God – *my* God!"

"*Our* gods," she said steadily in that tone of iron, "are near. The sacrifice is ready. And *you* – servant of mercy, priest of a younger deity, and English – you bring the power that makes it effectual. The circuit is complete."

It was perhaps the tears in her appealing eyes, perhaps it was her words, her voice, the wonder of her presence; all combined possibly in the spell that finally then struck down his will as with a single blow that paralysed his last resistance. The monstrous, half-legendary spirit of a primitive day recaptured him completely; he yielded to the spell of this tender, cruel woman, mother and avenging angel, whom horror and suffering had flung back upon the practices of uncivilized centuries. A common desire, a common lust and purpose, degraded both of them. They understood one another. Dropping back into a gulf of savage worship that set up idols in the place of God, they prayed to Odin and his awful crew . . .

It was again the touch of her hand that galvanized him. She raised him; he had been kneeling in slavish wonder and admiration at her feet. He leaped to do the bidding, however terrible, of this woman who was priestess, queen indeed, of a long-forgotten orgy.

"Vengeance at last!" he cried, in an exultant voice that no longer frightened him. "Now light the fire! Bring on the sacrifice!"

There was a rustling among the nearer branches, the forest stirred; the leaves of last year brushed against advancing feet. Yet before he could turn to see, before even the last words had wholly left his lips, the woman, whose hand still touched his fingers, suddenly tossed her cloak aside, and flinging her bare arms about his neck, drew him with impetuous passion towards her face and kissed him, as with delighted fury of exultant passion, full upon the mouth. Her body, in its clinging skins, pressed close against his own; her heat poured into him. She held him fiercely, savagely, and her burning kiss consumed his modern soul away with the fire of a primal day.

"The gods have given you to us," she cried, releasing him. "Your soul is ours!"

She turned – they turned together – to look for one upon whose last hour the moon now shed her horrid silver.

VIII

This silvery moonlight fell upon the scene.

Incongruously he remembered the flowers that soon would know the cuckoo's call; the soft mysterious stars shone down; the woods lay silent underneath the sky.

An amazing fantasy of dream shot here and there. "I am a man, an Englishman, a padre!" ran twisting through his mind, as though *she* whispered them to emphasize the ghastly contrast of reality. A memory of his own Kentish village with its Sunday school fled past, his dream of the Lion and the Lamb close after it. He saw children playing on the green . . . He saw their happy little hands . . .

Justice, punishment, revenge – he could not disentangle them. No longer did he wish to. The tide of violence was at his lips, quenching an ancient thirst. He drank. It seemed he could drink for ever. These tender pictures only sweetened horror. That kiss had burned his modern soul away.

The woman waved her hand; there swept from the underbrush a score of figures dressed like herself in skins, with leaves and flowers entwined among their flying hair. He was surrounded in a moment. Upon each face he noted the same tenderness and terrible resolve that their commander wore. They pressed about him, dancing with enchanting grace, yet with full-blooded abandon, across the chequered light and shadow. It was the brimming energy of their movements that swept him off his feet, waking the desire for fierce rhythmical expression. His own muscles leaped and ached; for this energy, it seemed, poured into him from the tossing arms and legs, the shimmering bodies whence hair and skins flung loose, setting the very air awhirl. It flowed over into inanimate objects even, so that the trees waved their branches although no wind stirred – hair, skins and hands, rushing leaves and flying fingers touched his face, his neck, his arms and shoulders, catching him away into this orgy of an ancient, sacrificial ritual. Faces with shining eyes peered into his, then sped away; grew in a cloud upon the moonlight; sank back in shadow; reappeared, touched him, whispered, vanished. Silvery limbs gleamed everywhere. Chanting rose in a wave, to fall away again into forest rustlings; there were smiles that flashed, then fainted into moonlight, red lips and gleaming teeth that shone, then faded out. The secret glade, picked from the heart of the forest by the moon, became a torrent of tumultuous life, a whirlpool of passionate emotions Time had not killed.

But it was the eyes that mastered him, for in their yearning, mating so incongruously with the savage grace – in the eyes shone ever tears. He was aware of gentle women, of womanhood, of accumulated feminine power that nothing could withstand, but of feminine power in majesty, its essential protective tenderness roused, as by tribal instinct, into a collective fury of implacable revenge. He was, above all, aware of motherhood – of mothers. And the man, the male, the father in him rose like a storm to meet it.

From the torrent of voices certain sentences emerged; sometimes chanted, sometimes driven into his whirling mind as though big whispers thrust them down his ears. "You are with us to the end," he caught. "We have the proof. And punishment is ours!"

It merged in wind, others took its place:

"We hold him fast. The old gods wait and listen."

The body of rushing whispers flowed like a storm-wind past.

A lovely face, fluttering close against his own, paused an instant, and starry eyes gazed into his with a passion of gratitude, dimming a moment their stern fury with a mother's tenderness: "For the little ones . . . it is necessary, it is the only way . . . Our own children . . ." The face went out in a gust of blackness, as the chorus rose with a new note of awe and reverence, and a score of throats uttered in unison a single cry: "The raven! The White Horses! His signs! Great Odin hears!"

He saw the great dark bird flap slowly across the clearing, and melt against the shadow of the giant beech; he heard its hoarse, croaking note; the crowds of heads bowed low before its passage. The White Horses he did not see; only a sound as of considerable masses of air regularly displaced was audible far overhead. But the veiled light, as though great thunder-clouds had risen, he saw distinctly. The sky above the clearing where he stood, panting and dishevelled, was blocked by a mass that owned unusual outline. These clouds now topped the forest, hiding the moon and stars. The flowers went out like nightlights blown. The wind rose slowly, then with sudden violence. There was a roaring in the tree-tops. The branches tossed and shook.

"The White Horses!" cried the voices, in a frenzy of adoration. "He is here!"

It came swiftly, this collective mass; it was both apt and terrible. There was an immense footstep. It was there.

Then panic seized him, he felt an answering tumult in himself, the Past surged through him like a sea at flood. Some inner sight, peering across the wreckage of To-day, perceived an outline that in its size dwarfed mountains, a pair of monstrous shoulders, a face that rolled through a full quarter of the heavens. Above the ruin of civilization, now fulfilled in the microcosm of his own being, the menacing shadow of a forgotten deity peered down upon the earth, yet upon one detail of it chiefly – the human group that had been wildly dancing, but that now chanted in solemn conclave about a forest altar.

For some minutes a dead silence reigned; the pouring winds left emptiness in which no leaf stirred; there was a hush, a stillness that could be felt. The kneeling figures stretched forth a level sea of arms towards the altar; from the lowered heads the hair hung down in torrents, against which the naked flesh shone white; the skins upon the rows of backs gleamed yellow. The obscurity deepened overhead. It was the time of adoration. He knelt as well, arms similarly outstretched, while the lust of vengeance burned within him.

Then came, across the stillness, the stirring of big wings, a rustling as the great bird settled in the higher branches of the beech. The ominous note broke through the silence; and with one accord the shining backs were straightened. The company rose, swayed, parting into groups and lines. Two score voices resumed the solemn chant. The throng of pallid faces passed to and fro like great fire-flies that shone and vanished. He, too, heard his own voice in unison, while his feet, as with instinctive knowledge, trod the same measure that the others trod.

Out of this tumult and clearly audible above the chorus and the rustling feet rang out suddenly, in a sweetly fluting tone, the leader's voice:

"The Fire! But first the hands!"

A rush of figures set instantly towards a thicket where the underbrush stood densest. Skins, trailing flowers, bare waving arms and tossing hair swept past on a burst of perfume. It was as though the trees themselves sped by. And the torrent of voices shook the very air in answer:

"The Fire! But first – the hands!"

Across this roaring volume pierced then, once again, that wailing sound which seemed both human and non-human – the anguished cry as of some lonely wolf in metamorphosis, apart from the collective safety of the pack, abjectly terrified, feeling the teeth of the final trap, and knowing the helpless feet within the steel. There was a crash of rending boughs and tearing branches. There was a tumult in the thicket, though of brief duration – then silence.

He stood watching, listening, overmastered by a diabolical sensation of expectancy he knew to be atrocious. Turning in the direction of the cry, his straining eyes seemed filled with blood; in his temples the pulses throbbed and hammered audibly. The next second he stiffened into a stone-like rigidity, as a figure, struggling violently yet half collapsed, was borne hurriedly past by a score of eager arms that swept it towards the beech tree, and then proceeded to fasten it in an upright position against the trunk. It was a man bound tight with thongs, adorned with leaves and flowers and trailing green. The face was hidden, for the head sagged forward on the breast, but he saw the arms forced flat against the giant trunk, held helpless beyond all possible escape; he saw the knife, poised and aimed by slender, graceful fingers above the victim's wrists laid bare; he saw the – hands.

"An eye for an eye," he heard, "a tooth for a tooth!" It rose in awful chorus. Yet this time, although the words roared close about him, they seemed farther away, as if wind brought them through the crowding trees from far off.

"Light the fire! Prepare the sacrifice!" came on a following wind; and, while strange distance held the voices as before, a new faint sound now audible was very close. There was a crackling. Some ten feet beyond the tree a column of thick smoke rose in the air; he was aware of heat not meant for modern purposes; of yellow light that was not the light of stars.

The figure writhed, and the face swung suddenly sideways. Glaring with panic hopelessness past the judge and past the hanging knife, the eyes found his own. There was a pause of perhaps five seconds, but in these five seconds centuries rolled by. The priest of To-day looked down into the well of time. For five hundred years he gazed into those twin eyeballs, glazed with the abject terror of a last appeal. They recognized one another.

The centuries dragged appallingly. The drama of civilization, in a sluggish stream, went slowly by, halting, meandering, losing itself, then reappearing. Sharpest pains, as of a thousand knives, accompanied its dreadful, endless lethargy. Its million hesitations made him suffer a million deaths of agony. Terror, despair and anger, all futile and without effect upon its progress, destroyed a thousand times his soul, which yet some hope – a towering, indestructible hope – a thousand times renewed. This despair and hope alternately broke his being, ever to fashion it anew. His torture seemed not of this world. Yet hope survived. The sluggish stream moved onward, forward . . .

There came an instant of sharpest, dislocating torture. The yellow light grew slightly brighter. He saw the eyelids flicker.

It was at this moment he realized abruptly that he stood alone, apart from the others, unnoticed apparently, perhaps forgotten; his feet held steady; his voice no longer sang. And at this discovery a quivering shock ran through his being, as though the will were suddenly loosened into a new activity, yet an activity that halted between two terrifying alternatives.

It was as though the flicker of those eyelids loosed a spring.

Two instincts, clashing in his being, fought furiously for the mastery. One, ancient as this sacrifice, savage as the legendary figure brooding in the heavens above him, battled fiercely with another, acquired more recently in human evolution, that had not yet crystallized into permanence. He saw a child, playing in a Kentish orchard with toys and flowers the little innocent hands made living . . . he saw a lowly manger, figures kneeling round it, and one star shining overhead in piercing and prophetic beauty.

Thought was impossible; he saw these symbols only, as the two contrary instincts, alternately hidden and revealed, fought for permanent possession of his soul. Each strove to dominate him; it seemed that violent blows were struck that wounded physically; he was bruised, he ached, he gasped for breath; his body swayed, held upright only, it seemed, by the awful appeal in the fixed and staring eyes.

The challenge had come at last to final action; the conqueror, he well knew, would remain an integral portion of his character, his soul.

It was the old, old battle, waged eternally in every human

heart, in every tribe, in every race, in every period, the essential principle indeed, behind the great world-war. In the stress and confusion of the fight, as the eyes of the victim, savage in victory, abject in defeat – the appealing eyes of that animal face against the tree stared with their awful blaze into his own, this flashed clearly over him. It was the battle between might and right, between love and hate, forgiveness and vengeance, Christ and the Devil. He heard the menacing thunder of "an eye for an eye, a tooth for a tooth", then above its angry volume rose suddenly another small silvery voice that pierced with sweetness: – "Vengeance is mine, I will repay . . ." sang through him as with unimaginable hope.

Something became incandescent in him then. He realized a singular merging of powers in absolute opposition to each other. It was as though they harmonized. Yet it was through this small, silvery voice the apparent magic came. The words, of course, were his own in memory, but they rose from his modern soul, now reawakening . . . He started painfully. He noted again that he stood apart, alone, perhaps forgotten of the others. The woman, leading a dancing throng about the blazing brushwood, was far from him. Her mind, too sure of his compliance, had momentarily left him. The chain was weakened. The circuit knew a break.

But this sudden realization was not of spontaneous origin. His heart had not produced it of its own accord. The unholy tumult of the orgy held him too slavishly in its awful sway for the tiny point of his modern soul to have pierced it thus unaided. The light flashed to him from an outside, natural source of simple loveliness – the singing of a bird. From the distance, faint and exquisite, there had reached him the silvery notes of a happy thrush, awake in the night, and telling its joy over and over again to itself. The innocent beauty of its song came through the forest and fell into his soul . . .

The eyes, he became aware, had shifted, focusing now upon an object nearer to them. The knife was moving.

There was a convulsive wriggle of the body, the head dropped loosely forward, no cry was audible. But, at the same moment, the inner battle ceased and an unexpected climax came. Did the soul of the bully faint with fear? Did his spirit leave him at the actual touch of earthly vengeance? The watcher never knew. In that appalling moment when the knife was about to begin the mission that the fire would complete, the roar of inner battle ended abruptly, and that small silvery voice drew the words of invincible power from his reawakening soul. "Ye do it also unto me ..." pealed o'er the forest.

He reeled. He acted instantaneously. Yet before he had dashed the knife from the hand of the executioner, scattered the pile of blazing wood, plunged through the astonished worshippers with a violence of strength that amazed even himself; before he had torn the thongs apart and loosened the fainting victim from the tree; before he had uttered a single word or cry, though it seemed to him he roared with a voice of thousands – he witnessed a sight that came surely from the Heaven of his earliest childhood days, from that Heaven whose God is love and whose forgiveness was taught him at his mother's knee.

With superhuman rapidity it passed before him and was gone. Yet it was no earthly figure that emerged from the forest, ran with this incredible swiftness past the startled throng, and reached the tree. He saw the shape; the same instant it was there; wrapped in light, as though a flame from the sacrificial fire flashed past him over the ground. It was of an incandescent brightness, yet brightest of all were the little outstretched hands. These were of purest gold, of a brilliance incredibly shining.

It was no earthly child that stretched forth these arms of generous forgiveness and took the bewildered prisoner by the hand just as the knife descended and touched the helpless wrists. The thongs were already loosened, and the victim, fallen to his knees, looked wildly this way and that for a way of possible escape, when the shining hands were laid upon his own. The murderer rose. Another instant and the throng must have been upon him, tearing him limb from limb. But the radiant little face looked down into his own; she raised him to his feet; with superhuman swiftness she led him through the infuriated concourse as though he had become invisible, guiding him safely past the furies into the cover of the trees. Close before his eyes, this happened; he saw the waft of golden brilliance, he heard the final gulp of it, as wind took the dazzling of its fiery appearance into space. They were gone . . .

IX

He stood, watching the disappearing motor-cars, wondering uneasily who the occupants were and what their business, whither and why did they hurry so swiftly through the night? He was still trying to light his pipe, but the damp tobacco would not burn.

The air stole out of the forest, cooling his body and his mind; he saw the anemones gleam; there was only peace and calm about him, the earth lay waiting for the sweet, mysterious stars. The moon was higher; he looked up; a late bird sang. Three strips of cloud, spaced far apart, were the footsteps of the South Wind, as she flew to bring more birds from Africa. His thoughts turned to gentle, happy hopes of a day when the lion and the lamb should lie down together, and a little child should lead them. War, in this haunt of ancient peace, seemed an incredible anachronism.

He did not go farther; he did not enter the forest; he turned back along the quiet road he had come, ate his food on a farmer's gate, and over a pipe sat dreaming of his sure belief that humanity had advanced. He went home to his hotel soon after midnight. He slept well, and next day walked back the four miles from the hospitals, instead of using the car. Another hospital searcher walked with him. They discussed the news.

"The weather's better anyhow," said his companion. "In our favour at last!"

"That's something," he agreed, as they passed a gang of prisoners and crossed the road to avoid saluting.

"Been another escape, I hear," the other mentioned. "He won't get far. How on earth do they manage it? The MO had a yarn that he was helped by a motor-car. I wonder what they'll do to him."

"Oh, nothing much. Bread and water and extra work, I suppose?"

The other laughed. "I'm not so sure," he said lightly. "Humanity hasn't advanced very much in that kind of thing."

A fugitive memory flashed for an instant through the other's brain as he listened. He had an odd feeling for a second that he had heard this conversation before somewhere. A ghostly sense of familiarity brushed his mind, then vanished. At dinner that night the table in front of him was unoccupied. He did not, however, notice that it was unoccupied.

www.ingramcontent.com/pod-product-compliance
Lightning Source LLC
Chambersburg PA
CBHW050311260626
47156CB00005B/1759